For my lively nephews, Sasha and Liam
—PJB

For my loved ones . . . the ones here and those over there!
—PB

DIAL BOOKS FOR YOUNG READERS • A division of Penguin Young Readers Group • Published by The Penguin Group • Penguin Group (USA) Inc., 375 Hudson Street, New York, NY 10014, U.S.A. • Penguin Group (Canada), 90 Eglinton Avenue East, Suite 700, Toronto, Ontario, Canada M4P 2Y3 (a division of Pearson Penguin Canada Inc.) • Penguin Books Ltd, 80 Strand, London WC2R 0RL, England • Penguin Ireland, 25 St. Stephen's Green, Dublin 2, Ireland (a division of Penguin Books Ltd) • Penguin Group (Australia), 250 Camberwell Road, Camberwell, Victoria 3124, Australia (a division of Pearson Australia Group Pty Ltd) • Penguin Books India Pvt Ltd, 11 Community Centre, Panchsheel Park, New Delhi - 110 017, India • Penguin Group (NZ), 67 Apollo Drive, Rosedale, North Shore 0632, New Zealand (a division of Pearson New Zealand Ltd) • Penguin Books (South Africa) (Pty) Ltd, 24 Sturdee Avenue, Rosebank, Johannesburg 2196, South Africa • Penguin Books Ltd, Registered Offices: 80 Strand, London WC2R 0RL, England • Text copyright © 2012 by P. J. Bracegirdle • Pictures copyright © 2012 by Poly Bernatene • All rights reserved • The publisher does not have any control over and does not assume any responsibility for author or third-party websites or their content. Designed by Jennifer Kelly • Text set in Green Std • Manufactured in China on acid-free paper
Library of Congress Cataloging-in-Publication Data available
10 9 8 7 6 5 4 3 2 1
The illustrations for this book were created digitally.

The Dead Family Diaz

by P. J. Bracegirdle

pictures by Poly Bernatene

DIAL BOOKS FOR YOUNG READERS
an imprint of Penguin Group (USA) Inc.

Morning came as the dead sun chased off the dead moon. All across the Land of the Dead, everyone's spirits were high.

"Rise and shine, sleepy skulls!" Mrs. Diaz called. "Breakfast is getting cold!"

"Huevos muertos!" cheered Estrellita. "Yum!"

Angelito looked at his plate miserably. Today was the Day of the Dead, when his family would walk among the Living. And Angelito was feeling scared.

"Did I tell you how the Living have big red tongues and bulging eyes?" his sister jabbered. "And if you touch one, they feel all hot and squishy!"

"Ew!" gasped Angelito, turning whiter than ever.

Mrs. Diaz hushed her daughter. "The Living are our friends," she said, "and this is the one time each year everyone gets together to celebrate."

But were they really hot and squishy? Angelito listened in horror to his sister's stories about Halloween, when the Living put out fiery-eyed pumpkins to scare the Dead away.

"Except it never works!" cackled Estrellita. "Mwahahahahahaha!!!"

"The Day of the Dead is nothing like Halloween," Angelito's father insisted. "Now eat up. We don't want to be late."

Angelito fed his breakfast to Dante while Estrellita chomped away. Finally the family piled into the car.

"I told you we should have left earlier," Mr. Diaz grumbled. "Just look at this traffic!"

Nearby, a large crowd was waiting for the elevator to the Land of the Living—and the Dead were getting restless.

"Quit pushing, numbskull!"

"Tell it to the zombies at the back!"

Jostled and shoved, the Diaz family squeezed into a packed elevator. Up and up they went, until—*ding!*—the doors finally opened.

"Welcome to the Land of the Living!" a booming voice shouted.

Pushed into the bright world beyond, Angelito froze.
Where were his parents? Shouting people, chiming bells,
and blaring music drowned out his calls. He darted
through the crowd, searching.

But his family was nowhere to be found.

Finally, Angelito arrived at a quiet square. Spotting a friendly looking skull, he asked, "You didn't see a man and a woman and a boneheaded girl wearing too much jaw-gloss pass by, did you?"

The boy laughed but shook his head. Angelito began to slump away.

"I'm Pablo, by the way," the boy called. "Did you happen to see any of *them* yet?"

Them? *He means the Living!* Angelito thought. He told Pablo all about the terrible shouting he'd heard near the elevators.

"They must be getting ready to attack," whispered Pablo. "Let's get out of here!"

The pair scrambled behind a fruit and vegetable stand, where Angelito came up with a plan: They'd tip over boxes of cherries so their enemies would slip.

"And then we can finish them off with these!" Pablo suggested, handing over a few tomatoes.

Before long, they heard an angry mob approaching.

"Get ready," whispered Angelito, "aim…"

"Wait! Hold your fire!" cried Pablo.

It wasn't a mob at all—but a parade full of banging drums and blasting trumpets! Still, Pablo warned that some of *them* might be hiding in it. "Maybe we should keep our masks on, just in case."

"Masks?" laughed the skeleton boy. "What masks?"

"These ones, silly," said Pablo, reaching for Angelito's face. "Hey, you're as cold as a Popsicle!" he squealed.

"And you've got bulging eyes!" cried Angelito.

"AAAAAAAH!

YOU'RE ONE OF *THEM!"*
they both shouted.

Angelito took off,
tearing down streets and
alleyways without looking back.

Out of breath, he finally stopped. Had
he really been playing with a Living boy
the whole time?

How freaky!
He shuddered.

How icky!
How awful!

But how incredibly fun,
he had to admit.

Except now he
was alone again.

Feeling glum, Angelito wandered around
the deserted town until he found himself
at the cemetery gates. Inside, a big party
was going on.

There was a loud bark.

"Dante!" Angelito cried,
rushing over to his family.

Mrs. Diaz squeezed her son so tightly, he thought he might crack. Angelito told them how he'd gotten lost and had been looking for them all day.

"We're just glad you're safe," sighed his father. "Now let's get to the buffet—I'm ready to stuff my rib cage!"

Estrellita slid up to her brother. "Oh, I bet you were *soooo* scared," she whispered gleefully. "All alone in the Land of the Living…"

"Actually, I wasn't alone," Angelito said.

And then, spotting a familiar face, the Dead boy discovered that he didn't need guts to be brave.

"Hey Pablo, wait up!" Angelito called.

The Living boy turned. Then a big smile crossed his face.

"Sorry for saying you had bulging eyes," said Angelito.

"Sorry for calling you a Popsicle," Pablo replied.

"So we're cool again?" Angelito asked, grinning a big skeleton grin.

Pablo winked. "Cool as your bones!"

Angelito told Pablo all the things Estrelita had said to make him scared of the Living. "She's okay mostly," he admitted, "but sometimes she can be a real knucklebone."

"Maybe she just needs to meet a real Living boy up close…" Pablo said.

The dead moon had already chased off the dead sun by the time the Dead family Diaz returned home.

Bone-tired, Angelito headed to bed, where he dreamed sweet dreams.

The Day of the Dead
(El Día de los Muertos)

is a holiday celebrated in Mexico on November first, when it is believed that the spirits of the dead return to visit the living. Though it is always sad when people die, the Day of the Dead is a happy holiday—a time for people to remember and appreciate friends and relatives who have passed on. The day is full of singing, dancing, and feasting. Special displays, known as altars, are made to welcome these beloved souls into the homes of their living family, with food laid out for the spirits to enjoy when they visit.